BEASTQUEST®

AMULET OF AVANTIA

→ BOOK TWENTY ←

EQUINUS
THE SPIRIT HORSE

ADAM BLADE

ILLUSTRATED BY EZRA TUCKER

SCHOLASTIC INC.

New York Toronto London Auckland
Sydney Mexico City New Delhi Hong Kong

With special thanks to Jan Burchett and Sara Vogler

For Timotej Torak with all good wishes

No part of this work may be reproduced, stored in a retrieval system, or transmitted in any form or by any means, electronic, mechanical, photocopying, recording, or otherwise, without written permission of the publisher. For information regarding permission, write to Working Partners Ltd., Stanley House, St Chad's Place, London WC1X 9HH, United Kingdom.

ISBN 978-0-545-27211-7

Beast Quest series created by Beast Quest Ltd., London. BEAST QUEST is a trademark of Beast Quest Ltd.

Text © 2009 by Beast Quest Ltd. All rights reserved.
Cover illustration © 2009 by Steve Sims
Interior illustrations © 2011 by Scholastic Inc.

Published by Scholastic Inc., 557 Broadway, New York, NY 10012, by arrangement with Working Partners Ltd.
SCHOLASTIC and associated logos are trademarks and/or registered trademarks of Scholastic Inc.

12 11 10 9 8 7 6 5 4 3 2 1   11 12 13 14 15 16/0

Designed by Tim Hall
Printed in the U.S.A.   40
First printing, July 2011

BEAST QUEST

→ ← ←

AMULET OF AVANTIA

BEASTQUEST®

CHARACTER GUIDE

HEROES AND VILLAINS

⇥ TOM ⇤

PREFERRED WEAPONS: Sword and magic shield

ALSO CARRIES: Destiny compass, jewel belt, and ghost map

SPECIAL SKILLS: Over the course of his Quest, Tom has gained many special items for his shield, giving him protection from fire, water, cold, and falling from heights, extra speed in battle, and magic healing ability. He also has the powers he gained from the golden armor, giving him incredible sight, courage, strength, endurance, sword skills, and energy.

⇥ Elenna ⇤

PREFERRED WEAPON: Bow & arrow

ALSO CARRIES: Nothing. Between her bow and
her wolf, Silver, Elenna doesn't need anything else!

SPECIAL SKILLS: Not only is Elenna an expert hunter,
she is also knowledgeable about boats and water.
But most important, she can think quickly in tight
spots, which has helped Tom more than once!

↦ STORM ↤

Tom's horse, a gift
from King Hugo.
Storm's good instincts
and speed have helped
Tom and Elenna from
the very beginning.

↦ SILVER ↤

Elenna's tame wolf and
constant companion. Not
only is Silver good to have
on their side in a fight,
but the wolf can also help
Tom and Elenna find
food when they're hungry.

⊹→ ADURO ←⊹

The good wizard of
Avantia and one of Tom's
closest allies. Aduro has
helped Tom many times,
but when Aduro was
captured by Malvel, Tom
was able to repay the
wizard by rescuing him.

⊹→ MALVEL ←⊹

Tom's enemy, determined
to enslave the Beasts of
Avantia and defeat Tom.
This evil wizard rules over
Gorgonia, the Dark
Realm. If he is near,
danger is sure to follow.

All hail, fellow followers of the Quest.

We have not met before but, like you, I have been watching Tom's adventures with a close eye. Do you know who I am? Have you heard of Taladon, the Master of the Beasts? I have returned — just in time for my son, Tom, to save me from a fate worse than death. The evil wizard, Malvel, has stolen something precious from me and until Tom is able to complete another Quest, I cannot be returned to full life. I must wait between worlds, neither human nor ghost. I am half the man I once was and only Tom can return me to my former glory.

Will Tom have the strength of heart to help his father? Another Quest can test even the most determined hero. And there may be a heavy price for my son to pay if he defeats six more Beasts. . . .

All I can do is hope — that Tom is successful. Will you put your power behind Tom and wish him well? I know I can count on my son — can I count on you, too? Not a moment can be wasted. As this latest Quest unfolds, much rides on it. We must all be brave.

Taladon

"Now it's your turn to give me a dare!" Jak told his friend Flint.

The boys were playing on the edge of their village. The sun had almost set over Errinel and heavy shadows were creeping across the ground. The sky was the color of a deep purple bruise, but the approaching darkness just made their game of Dare even better. Flint looked around, and Jak saw his eyes light up as he pointed toward some trees in a nearby field.

"Dare you to snatch an apple from Farmer Grindall's orchard," said Flint.

"No problem!" Jak vaulted over a wooden fence, strolled into the orchard, and climbed up the tallest apple tree. He'd show Flint he wasn't scared — even though grumpy old Farmer Grindall would chase him with a stick if he saw him.

As he reached the top branch, he had a good view of the road that led away from the village and ran alongside the boundary of Avantia, King Hugo's kingdom. It was marked by a high, forbidding wall with an old iron gate, but even from his position in the tree, Jak couldn't see over it. Beyond the wall was the Forbidden Land. Jak knew that no one ever went near that place. The other villagers wouldn't even talk about it. But looking at the black, sinister wall gave him an idea for the best dare ever!

He plucked an apple, swung down from the tree, and jumped back over the fence.

"You win that one," admitted Flint, as Jak tossed him the apple.

"Now here's your next dare," said Jak. "It's so frightening I bet you won't do it."

"Nothing's too frightening for me!" Flint said confidently.

"I dare you to go into the Forbidden Land!" challenged Jak. He folded his arms, sure that his friend would admit defeat.

But Flint didn't say a word. Instead he strode down the road to the gate in the wall.

Jak ran after him, his heart beating hard. "You don't have to do it," he called. "It was just a joke."

"I *never* say no to a dare," said Flint as he grasped the ironwork and began to climb.

"Then I'm coming with you." The gate was rusty and felt unstable beneath Jak's grip as he scrambled up it. He climbed on. He couldn't let his friend go alone.

The boys were soon sitting astride the gate, staring in amazement at the sight before them. The Forbidden Land was gray as far as the eye could see. The ground was covered with a thick layer of dust and the only trees that grew nearby were blackened and gnarled.

"It's horrible!" Flint said with a gasp.

"Everything is so dead looking," murmured Jak in reply.

They slid to the ground of the Forbidden Land and walked slowly away from the gate. Their boots left deep prints in the ashlike powder. Jak saw his friend shiver.

"We've done the dare," Flint said. His voice sounded odd and flat in this strange place, and the gate suddenly seemed a long way away. "Let's get back."

Jak nodded, but suddenly spotted something on the horizon. "What's that?"

Flint followed his gaze. "It looks like a dust cloud." His face looked worried and he glanced down at his feet. "Can you feel the ground?"

Jak could. The gray earth beneath their feet was vibrating and sending shudders up their legs.

"Something's coming," he whispered. The boys stood transfixed as the cloud of dust got nearer and the vibrations coming from the ground became stronger.

"It's a horse!" Flint exclaimed, peering into the distance. "And it's big."

Jak looked hard. His friend was right. He could just make out a glint of hooves and he realized that the hoofbeats must be causing the vibrations. He caught a glimpse of a man sitting tall in the saddle.

"I wonder who the rider is," he said as the horse got closer. "No, wait . . ." With rising horror, he saw that the man's body was joined to the horse. It was some kind of Beast — part man, part horse. But the Beasts didn't exist, did they? They were just made-up stories of Avantia that Jak repeated when he wanted to scare his little brother.

The Beast suddenly became transparent and Jak felt his jaw drop open in shock.

"I can see right through him." Flint swallowed

nervously. "He's a ghost. And he's coming straight at us!"

Jak and Flint dashed for the gate, their feet churning up the gray dust. The Beast was getting closer, but the boys were fast runners. *We're going to make it*, Jak thought with relief. But just as they got to the wall, Flint tripped and fell, sprawling into the dust.

Jak quickly helped him stand, but above their heads came an almighty roar. The friends looked up. The Beast, solid once again, was on top of them and rearing up on his hind legs, ready to crush them. Jak gazed at the Beast and saw an expression of joy and delight etched onto his skeleton-like face.

The boys were paralyzed with fear and screamed as the terrifying Beast lunged down. Jak felt an icy cold feeling sweeping over his whole body and gasped as he realized that the Beast had turned ghostly again and had somehow passed straight through him. Tears of despair trickled down Jak's face as he felt something being torn from him. He forced himself to look at Flint. His friend stood pale and expressionless.

With his last thought, Jak knew what had happened to them both. The Beasts were real, after all. And this one had taken their life force. . . .

→ CHAPTER ONE ←

A NEW DANGER

Tom MADE HIS WAY THROUGH THE MINE tunnels with Elenna close by his side. He could see daylight ahead. Only moments before, they had defeated Nixa the Death Bringer, one of Malvel's evil Ghost Beasts, and Tom was glad to be leaving the dark and the memories of the shape-shifter behind.

"We'll soon be out of here," declared Elenna, tightening the coil of rope around her waist. "And the sooner, the better."

"It was a hard Quest," said Tom. "But we won in the end."

"And we've got back the first piece of the amulet for your father," said Elenna with a grin. "I know we've got five more to go, but it's a good start."

"My father looked stronger already when he appeared to us just now, didn't he?" Tom asked eagerly.

Elenna nodded.

Tom felt a surge of happiness. He had grown up not knowing whether his father, Taladon, was alive or dead, but two days ago Tom had come face-to-face with him. He'd discovered that his father was a ghost stranded between the real world and the spirit realm. Malvel's evil magic had done this, and the only way to make Taladon flesh and blood again was to locate the six pieces of the Amulet of Avantia and fit them all together. This was Tom's Quest, but it would not be easy to recover the amulet fragments because each of them was guarded by one of Malvel's Ghost Beasts.

Tom touched the first piece of the amulet that hung from the leather cord around his neck. Taladon had told them that the second piece was guarded by Equinus the Spirit Horse.

"Father said Equinus would be a dangerous foe," Tom commented. "But we won't let that stop us."

"No, we won't," Elenna said determinedly. "Look, we're leaving the mines at last!" They ran out of the tunnel.

As they blinked in the sunlight, they heard a friendly whinny and a happy howl. Storm, Tom's stallion, and Silver, Elenna's wolf, came charging over to them.

"Thank you for waiting so patiently," Tom said to Storm as he stroked the horse's glossy black neck.

"I think they're glad to see us!" Elenna laughed. Silver was jumping around her in circles excitedly.

"Now that the team's all together, we can start our next Quest." Tom held out his hand. "Map," he called.

The air in front of them shimmered and the map that Aduro had given to Tom materialized. They would have to fight Ghost Beasts — so the map itself was ghostly. It hung in the air before them, showing the whole dusty, gray Forbidden Land.

"We're here." Elenna pointed to the rocky mouth of the mine on the map.

"And that's the way we must go!" exclaimed Tom, as a glowing path appeared that led in a straight line across the map and into a tangled knot of trees. "To that forest in the east." Tom stared at the trees on the map. They looked dark and forbidding. He knew that somewhere among those trunks lurked Equinus.

Tom flicked open the brass lid of the compass that his father had given him. He did not need to look to remember the words inscribed on the bottom: *For My Son*. They always filled him with a warm glow. He located east on the navigational instrument and pointed in that direction. "We have a long journey ahead of us," he said. "It'll be quicker if we ride." He swung up onto Storm's back and held out a hand to Elenna.

"The beginning of another adventure!" cried Elenna as she climbed up behind him. She sounded excited, but Tom could sense that she had the same fears as he did. The two friends had already met many fearsome and terrifying Beasts on their Quests.

What new terrors awaited them now?

⤙ Chapter Two ⤚

Through the Dead Land

"**I** wonder what Equinus will be like," said Elenna as they cantered along, Silver bounding eagerly at Storm's heels. They had traveled a long way from the mine, but the land was still just as flat and gray in all directions.

"Equinus can't be worse than Nixa the Death Bringer," Tom answered. "She was one of the most devious Beasts that we've ever met." He peered ahead across the plain. On his Quest to save a good Beast, Sepron the Sea Serpent, from the clutches of Malvel, Tom had been given a golden helmet with the gift of wonderfully sharp eyesight. He no longer had the helmet, but the ability had remained with him. However, there was no sign of the forest they were heading for, just more dull, gray land with one or two ashen bushes and solitary trees here and there.

"This isn't the most cheerful place we've ever been," said Elenna. "Even the sunshine doesn't feel warm."

Tom looked up. The sky was bright, but it was a cold, dead light, and the air was heavy with a stale and musty smell.

"I don't think we've ever been anywhere as desolate," he said. "Gorgonia was frightening, but this is just so . . . empty."

"Nothing but dust," agreed Elenna. "Poor Silver's getting covered in it." She leaned down to her pet wolf. "Sorry, boy. Wish you could ride with us, but there's not enough room!"

Silver sneezed and shook himself, throwing out gray clouds all around him.

They rode on.

"I can see treetops!" Tom said suddenly. He reined in Storm and looked intently into the distance. "It must be the forest."

"At last!" exclaimed Elenna.

He squeezed Storm's flanks with his legs, and the stallion snorted and set off at a gallop. Silver bounded ahead.

But as they neared the trees, Storm's pace slowed to a trot and Silver hung back. Tom tried urging Storm to go faster, but the stallion would take only anxious steps forward, glancing nervously to the left and right. Tom felt Elenna's grip tighten around his waist. She was apprehensive as well. He put his hand to his sword and felt its strength. He knew he must be strong, too. If there was a Beast waiting for them here, when might it appear? Was Equinus hiding in the shelter of the trees?

As if in answer to Tom's unspoken question, an ear-piercing scream split the air.

→ CHAPTER THREE ←

CHARGE OF THE GHOST BEAST

Storm reared up at the terrifying sound, his front hooves flying. Tom and Elenna clung on as the stallion bucked and twisted in terror.

Then Tom vaulted quickly out of the saddle. "Hold on tight!" he shouted to Elenna. "I'll try to calm him down." Dodging the flailing hooves, he leaped at Storm's bridle and gripped it hard.

The stallion's nostrils were flared and his flanks heaved. It took all Tom's strength to hold on to the terrified horse, and he could see that Elenna was only just managing to remain seated. Tom stroked Storm's head and spoke to him soothingly, and almost instantly the horse began to settle.

Elenna slipped from the stallion's back, looking stunned.

"Thanks, Tom," she said. Silver creeped to her. Hackles rising, he cowered at her feet, growling softly.

"What could have made that noise?" said Elenna with a shiver. "It sounded as if it was coming from the trees."

"I don't know," answered Tom. "But whatever it is, we must be ready for it."

Just then, Elenna gave a cry of warning as a huge shape, shrouded in a cloud of dust, came crashing out of the trees.

Tom looked more closely. It was a Beast. He had the torso of a man and the body of a horse, and was heading straight for them. "Equinus!" Tom breathed.

"He's just like Tagus!" Elenna said. "But much bigger."

As the cloud of dust parted, Tom could see who he was facing more clearly. The sight made his blood run cold. Even from this distance, he could see the evil flashing in Equinus's blazing eyes. The Beast's long brown hair lashed the air behind him, and his hideous skeletal face was parched dry, like the land all around them.

Elenna put a reassuring hand on Silver's back. He whimpered, pressing hard against her leg. Meanwhile, Tom struggled to hold on to Storm's bridle — the terrified stallion was tossing his head and trying to pull away.

Tom felt the ground vibrating beneath his feet as the Beast galloped toward them, churning up great clouds of dust. The force of his pounding hooves broke apart the dry earth and cracks snaked toward them and spread out around their feet.

"Get behind me, Elenna." Tom gave her Storm's reins and drew his sword.

He frowned as he saw that the Beast's form was changing. One minute Equinus was solid, his skin the color of cold ivory and his flank an ashen gray, but the next Tom could see the forest through his body. Tom realized that Equinus could take either a solid or a ghostly form when he wished, just like Nixa — and that made him a most dangerous enemy. As the Beast drew closer, Tom saw the spirit horse's heart throbbing in his chest. He felt a new thrill of horror run through him. This was no ordinary heart. This heart was as black as night.

Tom knew that he must not let his friends face such a foe. Controlling his own rising fear, he held up his wooden shield. It gleamed with the six tokens given to him by the good Beasts of Avantia. Each token had helped protect him on his Quests, and the thought gave him the courage he needed now.

"While there is blood in my veins I will not fail in my Quest!" he shouted. Swishing the sword fiercely above his head, he leaped forward to meet the Beast. But as he charged, he realized that he was not alone. Silver was running alongside him, barking wildly, and Elenna was on his other side, bow and arrow ready in her hands. Tom's heart leaped as he caught sight of his brave stallion galloping ahead. They had all come to help him.

Equinus had taken his solid form again now. His mighty bulk reared up in front of Tom. Gripping his sword tightly in both hands, Tom made a great arc in the air just as Equinus came down toward him. The Beast dodged the sword and landed with a clattering of hooves. Equinus turned to face him again. There was a sudden, terrible silence. The Beast's blazing eyes bored into Tom's and one of his giant hooves pawed the ground like a bull, ready to charge.

Slowly, they began to circle each other. Sword at the ready, Tom kept his eyes fixed on his enemy. Looking at the Beast's heaving chest and massive

muscles, Tom could see that strength alone would not be enough to defeat him. He knew that Elenna was standing a little way back with Storm and Silver at her side, but he sensed that even the four of them might not be a match for this mighty enemy.

Equinus's eyes were bloodred with evil hatred and he tossed his head from side to side angrily. Suddenly, he lunged forward, and Tom only just managed to beat him back with fierce thrusts from his sword. Tom pressed his advantage but caught his foot on a root, stumbled, and fell. The Beast reared up, foam flying from his snarling lips. Elenna cried out in alarm, and Tom saw her shoot an arrow at the flank of the Beast. It bounced off harmlessly, but it was enough to distract Equinus. The Beast now turned to face Elenna.

Tom leaped to his feet. He knew he had to act quickly. This was his chance to plunge his sword deep into the black heart of the Beast. He sized up his enemy. Equinus was tall, so Tom got ready to use the magic jumping ability that would allow him to leap up and strike. He crouched, ready to spring, waiting to feel the surge of strength that usually coursed through his legs. Nothing happened! He tried again. Still nothing.

Equinus still had his eyes fixed on Elenna, Storm, and Silver. His thin lips parted in a horrible snarl and he let out a sharp cry of evil laughter. He reared up and began to gallop toward Tom's friends.

"No!" Tom yelled at the top of his voice. Fury surged through his veins. He was not going to let his friends be hurt — or worse. Tom started to run.

Elenna fired off more arrows, but Equinus would not be halted. Instead he changed his direction slightly and charged straight toward Storm. The stallion seemed transfixed with terror and did not move.

Tom ran even faster. Equinus reared up and Tom could see that the Beast was about to crush poor Storm. Elenna gave a shriek of fear as she joined Tom in the desperate dash toward the stallion. But they were too late. Equinus gave a cruel cry of mocking laughter as he crashed down on top of Storm.

CHAPTER FOUR

TOM'S CHOICE

"STORM!" SHOUTED TOM, HIS VOICE HOARSE. Suddenly, he saw the Beast flicker and change into his ghostly form, and instead of crushing Storm, he charged straight through him. The air around the horse and Beast shuddered, giving off a harsh silver light. Tom felt the force of it pushing him backward. Silver bowed his head and Elenna held up her hands to shield herself from the blazing light. Tom saw Storm drop to his knees.

Equinus now veered around. Tom saw that his evil black heart had swelled in his chest and pounded more strongly than before. The Beast gave a shriek of triumph, and every angle on his mocking skeletal face stood out sharp and cruel. Then he galloped off toward the forest, churning the dust around him as he went. In an instant, he had vanished.

Tom stared at Storm. He could see that his friend was taking in deep, shuddering breaths. He was still alive! Tom raced over to him, Elenna close behind. But even before Tom reached Storm he knew that something was wrong. The stallion was making no effort to stand up. Tom took the horse's bridle and helped him to his feet. He stroked him soothingly, but Storm stood silent and seemed unable to take a step forward. Even when Tom flung his arms around Storm's neck, the black stallion made no sign that he recognized his friend.

"Storm, it's me," whispered Tom, stroking the horse's neck. "It's okay. The Beast has gone. You're safe."

"I think something's happened to him, Tom." Elenna looked distressed. "His eyes are . . . strange."

Tom gazed deep into Storm's brown eyes. "They're dead!" he said with a gasp. "It's like looking at a stone carving. Oh, Storm, I've failed you. What has Equinus done?"

Elenna buried her face in Storm's mane. Silver whined at her feet.

"I think I can explain," came a voice.

Tom and Elenna whirled around at the sound. A soft golden glow filled the air and a vision of Taladon appeared. He stared gravely at them and then looked at Storm, who was still gazing sightlessly into the distance.

"Tell me quickly!" demanded Tom. "What's happened to my friend?"

Taladon bowed his head in sorrow. "Equinus does not kill. He does something even more evil. He feeds on the spirits of other creatures and leaves them to a dismal, cheerless life forever after. He has taken Storm's spirit. I am so sorry. I did not think this would happen."

Tom remembered how Equinus's heart had grown larger after his attack on Storm. Now he understood. It had swelled thanks to Storm's stolen life force. Suddenly, he was full of rage — and not just against Equinus. His insides were alive with anger against his father, too. "If you knew all about this, why didn't you tell me it could happen?" he shouted at him, fists clenched. "I would never have let my friends be exposed to such danger."

"You are right, my son," said Taladon quietly. "I knew about the power of Equinus and I should have warned you."

"Then you have done a terrible thing!" Tom almost choked on the words.

Elenna took his arm. "Don't, Tom," she pleaded. "I'm sure Taladon can explain."

"I hope so, Elenna," Tom's father said in the same quiet tone. "You see, I was convinced that you'd be able to use one of your many powers to overcome Equinus, but I was wrong to think that. I was wrong to expect that."

Tom stared hard at his father. "What do you mean?"

"It weakens me each time I appear to you like this. But I must show you something." Taladon held out his hand and made a movement in the air. A vision immediately materialized in front of Tom and Elenna. Tom started in surprise. There before them was an image of the rearing Equinus. Silver gave a low growl and stood in front of Elenna as if to protect her.

"Look carefully," Taladon told Tom. "This will help you understand."

As he spoke, Tom himself appeared in the vision. Now Tom realized what his father was showing him. It was the struggle he had just had with Equinus. He saw himself brandishing his sword and trying to leap at the Beast's black heart. It filled him with horror to relive the terrible moment: to see himself crouched and ready for the giant leap — and then find that he was unable to do so. A feeling of utter helplessness flooded over him again as, in the vision, he saw Equinus charge at Storm and pass through him.

Taladon raised a hand and the vision was gone. Elenna had tears running down her face. She wiped them away, as if she didn't want Tom to see. Tom swallowed down his own grief for the noble stallion who was lost to him forever. What good were his Quests without Storm by his side?

"I failed," said Tom brokenly. "Why are you reminding me of it?"

Taladon shook his head. "It was not your failure, my son," he said, looking kindly at him. "Something happened that you could not overcome."

Tom shot a questioning glance at his father.

"Let me explain," Taladon went on. "You took on the task of finding the six pieces of my amulet — and I cannot tell you how proud I am that you were brave enough to accept the challenge. But I would not have let you set out if I had known the true price of your Quest." He paused for a moment. "You see, with each piece of the amulet that you recover, one of the magic powers granted by the golden armor will return to its true master . . . me. Your armor was once mine, and its powers are returning my strength."

"That's why you couldn't leap!" exclaimed Elenna. "The moment we defeated Nixa and won back the first piece of your father's amulet, the power from your golden boots must have returned to Taladon."

Tom's father nodded. "Now, son, I need to ask you a question, and I want you to think very seriously before you answer it." He looked intently at Tom. "I would not for the world put you and your companions in more peril. And there will surely be danger ahead of you. Do you wish to continue with this Quest?"

Tom looked deep into his father's eyes. If he gave up now, Taladon would be a ghost forever. If he was to become flesh and blood again, the six pieces of the amulet must be recovered. And only Tom could do that. He raised his sword high in the air. "While there is blood in my veins I will complete my Quest!"

CHAPTER FIVE

TIME IS RUNNING OUT

"I KNEW YOU WOULD NOT GIVE UP, TOM," said Taladon with a smile.

As he spoke, the air around him seemed to glow brightly, sending its warmth deep into Tom's heart. His father was proud of him, and that was enough. But then a stab of pain shot through him as he remembered Storm, who was now nothing but an empty shell and refused to move. Tom would have no choice but to leave his poor horse while he completed his Quest.

As if he knew what Tom was thinking, Taladon spoke briskly. "There's no time to lose, but there is something I must show you first. Look at your compass."

Puzzled, Tom flicked open the compass lid.

Taladon smiled. "Your compass has a hidden secret."

Tom stared at the instrument's bobbing needle. *What secret could it possibly have?*

"Run your finger around the outside of the case," Taladon told him. "There is a concealed button. Can you feel it?"

Tom did as his father asked. At first he could feel only the cold, smooth brass under his fingers. But then his finger felt a tiny raised circle that he had not noticed before. He pressed it, and the face of the compass immediately flicked open.

"What's inside?" Elenna was looking eagerly over Tom's shoulder.

"It's a sort of clock!" gasped Tom. He stared at the little face with its finely painted numbers around the rim. The clock had a single hand in the shape of a delicate golden arrow. The pointed head was slowly inching its way around.

"It's been hidden away all this time and we never knew!" exclaimed Elenna. "It doesn't seem to tell the time, though." She looked at Taladon questioningly.

"Not in the usual way," agreed Taladon. "But it tells you something much more important. This golden hand starts at the top of the clock at twelve, and travels around once. It tells you when time is running out to complete a Quest or to right a wrong."

"It's already well on its way around!" cried Tom.

"Yes, the hand began to move the moment that Equinus took away Storm's spirit." Taladon's voice was growing fainter now and his image was fading. "But as you can see, there is still time to save your friend."

"But how?" Tom asked desperately. He wanted to hold on to his father and keep his ghostly image with him, but he knew it was impossible.

"You must defeat Equinus before the hand reaches twelve again." Taladon's voice was a distant whisper now. "If you do this, Storm will get his spirit back. If you fail, he will be lifeless forever."

Tom looked at Elenna with sudden hope. Elenna's eyes were gleaming, and Tom knew she had the same thought he did.

"We're going to save Storm!" he whispered.

"We just need to find a way to defeat that horrible Beast," answered Elenna.

"We've never failed before," declared Tom. "And we won't this time. But we need help."

He whirled around to his father. But the vision was gone. Tom and Elenna were alone.

Elenna took Tom by the shoulders. "You can do this!" she urged him. "For your father — and for Storm."

Tom nodded gravely. "Storm must stay here," he said firmly. "He can't defend himself without his life force. If he comes with us, he'll be in terrible danger."

He gathered Storm's reins to tie to a nearby oak tree. Its bark was pale and its leaves thin and papery. As Tom tossed the reins over a low branch, acorns tumbled around him and crumbled to dust. Elenna came to his side, with Silver at her heels.

"I'll leave Silver to guard him." She bent down and patted the wolf's thick coat. "You must stay here and look after Storm," she told him. "We will be back as soon as we can."

Silver seemed to understand. He gave the stallion a friendly nudge and then took a bold stance next to him.

"He won't let us down." Elenna smiled.

Silver gave Elenna's hand an eager lick, but Storm stood motionless as the two friends said good-bye to him. Tom wrenched his gaze away from his horse and turned resolutely toward the dreaded forest.

As they headed for the trees, Tom couldn't help but conjure up in his mind the image of the hidden clock. *How far has the hand gone around?* He wanted to keep checking but knew he must concentrate on the task at hand — and not waste time worrying.

Suddenly, Elenna stopped in her tracks. "Tom!" she cried. "Those trees ahead don't look like they are part of an ordinary forest. It's a rain forest."

Tom halted as well. He had been so busy worrying about Storm that he hadn't paid attention to the changing environment. He took in the dense tangle of huge leaves and creepers.

"Well, that's the way Equinus went, so that's the way we're going," he declared.

They strode boldly into the jungle. The trees were close together, their thick branches stretching toward the sky as if they were fighting for the light.

The trunks were suffocated with vines and ivy. Everything was parched and gray.

"We've never seen a jungle quite like this," Elenna said, reaching out to push aside a creeper. It turned to powder at her touch. "It's all dead," she said, coughing in the dusty air. "Just like the rest of the Forbidden Land."

Tom strode into the tangle, crushing the knee-high undergrowth as he went. His shoulder brushed against a massive tree trunk and bark peeled away.

"Ugh!" exclaimed Elenna, following in his wake as they drove deeper into the jungle. "This ash is clinging to my legs. It's horrible!"

"The air is thick with it," agreed Tom. "It's hard to even breathe. I just hope this is the right path."

As if in answer, Tom's ghostly map appeared in front of them, glowing in the half-light that filtered through the dense foliage. There on the map was the rain forest, and deep within the trees was a tiny image of Equinus with a path leading straight to him.

"Looks as if we've just got to keep going," said Elenna grimly, as the map faded. "It won't be long before we find him — or he finds us. . . ."

"I hope he *does* seek us out. The sooner we find him, the sooner we can defeat him," said Tom. "We need to save Storm."

"We'll save him. Equinus doesn't stand a chance against the both of us," declared Elenna.

Tom threw her a look of gratitude. Elenna's friendship was the best gift he had. He struck out again through the undergrowth, with Elenna a few steps behind. But he had not gone far when he heard Elenna cry out.

"Get off!" she screamed.

Tom swung around, his sword drawn, expecting to see Equinus. Instead, he saw Elenna standing by a fallen log. It looked as if she was covered in a sea of whitish, moving slime that started at her ankles and was working its way up her body. She was slapping wildly at her clothes.

What's going on? Tom thought. He was about to leap to her aid when he felt a creepy sensation crawling up his legs.

He looked down to see a seething mass of huge, writhing maggots!

CHAPTER SIX

THE EVIL WIND

TOM THRASHED ABOUT, BRUSHING THE HORRID, squirming creatures off his clothes and skin. The maggots were a putrid, sickly white color and each was as big as a clenched fist. They had hungry-looking mouths.

"They're disgusting!" Elenna said, pulling at her tunic and shaking it. Some maggots fell off, but more were already crawling up from the dusty undergrowth.

"At least *something* is alive in this dreadful place," Tom said grimly. He quickly ran through his magical abilities in his head, but couldn't think of anything that would help get rid of the slimy creepy-crawlies. "We'll just have to keep moving. That way, no more will be able to climb onto us."

"Then let's go!" insisted Elenna with a shudder. "And fast. Before they decide that we might be worth eating."

They rushed through the knee-high dust, scattering the clinging maggots as they went. All the time, Tom looked this way and that for signs of Equinus.

"It doesn't make sense," said Tom, as they pushed through the decaying giant leaves and creepers of the jungle. "Why would Equinus choose to live here? Horses don't belong in jungles — even a Ghost Beast who is part horse and part man!"

"I don't know," Elenna said. "But the map led us here. We have to keep going and look out for any clues that lead us to Equinus and the amulet. And quickly."

Tom understood her urgency. Time was running out for Storm. He stared all around them. "Hey, wait a minute!" They were standing by a tall tree that was so high the top was lost in the jungle canopy. Tom pointed at its trunk. "Look at this!" he cried. There were deep, crescent-shaped grooves high in the crumbling bark. "These marks were made by hooves. I'm sure of it." He stretched up, but couldn't reach them. "They're too far above the ground to have been made by an ordinary horse."

"Equinus!" said Elenna excitedly. "It must have been. He's big enough to reach that high. But why would he have been kicking at this tree?" Her brow creased with concentration; then her eyes lit up. "Tom, remember what Aduro told us? The Beasts don't just guard the pieces of amulet — they hide them."

Tom felt himself grinning as he realized what Elenna was telling him. "Equinus wasn't kicking the tree," he said. "He wanted to hide something up there, and so must have been rearing up on his hind legs and leaning his front hooves on the trunk. For all that effort, he must have been hiding something very precious."

"The piece of amulet!" breathed Elenna.

Tom nodded and strapped his shield to his back. "I may have lost my magic ability to leap up high," he told Elenna, "but I can still climb trees!"

He began to clamber up the trunk, but the crumbling bark made it very hard to get a grip. He gritted his teeth and pushed onward.

"You're not the only one who can climb trees." Tom looked down and saw Elenna following him. He was glad. He had the feeling he was going to need all the help he could get.

As they climbed, they carefully scanned the branches for any sign of the amulet. They rested on a thick bough about a third of the way up and Tom flicked open the compass.

"The hand's already halfway around," he said in frustration. Then he straightened his shoulders. He knew that getting upset wouldn't save Storm. "We'd better keep on moving."

They climbed up and up until the ground seemed a very long way down.

"We must be at the hiding place," said Tom. "Look, the hoof marks don't reach this far."

"Check the branches and the trunk," said Elenna. "Whoa!" She flung her arms tightly around the trunk as the tree began to shake. Tom clutched desperately to the tree as well.

A sudden wind had sprung up. It circled the tree, tugging at their clothes and making the branches shudder. It howled and whistled with a strange, unearthly noise.

"The wind sounds like it's laughing," said Elenna, as she struggled to keep her hold on the decaying bark.

"It *is* laughing," Tom said, through gritted teeth. "This is no ordinary wind. I think it's been sent by Malvel to stop us." He gripped the tree even more tightly. "Blow all you like!" he shouted into the powerful breeze. "We'll never give up. We're going to find the amulet piece!"

The tree began to sway more violently, crashing against its neighbors. Branches fell about Tom's head. Bark was being stripped from under his fingers by the evil tornado, and Tom felt his feet slip. For a moment, he held on with his arms alone. If he lost his grip, he would knock into Elenna and send her plunging to the ground with him. He knew *he* would land safely if he fell — Cypher's tear in his shield would make sure of that, but it wouldn't help Elenna. Tom searched for a foothold with the toe of his boot and, at last, found one.

"I don't know how much longer I can hold on," Elenna shouted up to him.

"You can't let go," Tom yelled back above the evil, screeching roar. "We're too high. You won't survive the fa —" He broke off in shock, as Elenna seemed to suddenly lose her grip on the tree.

→ CHAPTER SEVEN ←

TERROR IN THE TREES

Tom's HEART POUNDED FIERCELY IN HIS CHEST, but he breathed a sigh of relief as he saw that his friend was gripping the tree trunk tightly with her legs and had let go with her hands so she could pull an arrow from her quiver.

"I've got an idea!" she told him quickly. "It'll keep us both safe."

She untied the rope from around her waist and fixed it to the feathered end of the arrow. Tom was impressed that Elenna managed to tie a knot while the dreadful wind shook the tree fiercely.

"I'm going to shoot this arrow deep into that branch," she said, pointing up to a thicker, sturdier limb higher up in the tree. "Hopefully it will hold firm, and then we can tie ourselves to the rope. That way we won't fall."

"Brilliant plan!" exclaimed Tom.

She pulled the bowstring back and aimed the arrow at the top of the tree. The arrow shot upward, and Elenna's aim was true.

Tom gave the dangling rope a hard yank. "It's holding!" he said. "Well done, Elenna!"

He tied a loop of the rope around his waist and handed the end to his friend so that she could do the same. The shrieking wind was so strong now that it seemed to snatch the breath out of Tom's mouth as he pulled himself up the tree. Elenna was right behind him.

And then Tom saw a patch of bark that looked different from the rest of the tree — uneven and protruding.

"Here!" he shouted to Elenna. "This part's been pulled off and then rammed back in."

"Peel it off, Tom," she said eagerly.

Bracing himself against the wind, he worked at the bark with his fingertips. "It's coming away!" he yelled. The bark came loose and tumbled to the ground far below. Tom peered inside the hole. There, glowing brightly within the decaying tree, was a jagged piece of silver with a blue enamel inset.

"It's the second piece of amulet!" cried Tom in triumph. He gently put his hand into the hole and picked it up. It seemed to shine even more brightly in his grasp, although the wind threatened to pluck it away. Tom showed his precious discovery to Elenna before safely putting it in his tunic pocket.

"Let's get down," Elenna said.

Untying the rope from their waists, they held on to the end as they bounced down the trunk in huge bounds until they were back on the firm, dusty jungle floor. Tom then used his super-strength to pull the rope, and the firmly embedded arrowhead fell from the branch high above their heads.

Elenna tied the rope back around her waist. "Right, let's get going. We've finished one part of our Quest, but we still have a Ghost Beast to find."

But before they had a chance to move on, they heard a terrible creak behind them, and then the sound of fracturing wood. They both looked up and saw the massive tree that they'd just climbed toppling toward them.

"Watch out!" yelled Tom. They dove out of the way just as the tree hit the ground, missing them by a hairbreadth. The wind gusted madly around them for a moment and, with a final howl of fury, blew away.

The jungle was suddenly silent again. "Looks like Malvel has given up," Tom said with a grin as he and his friend staggered to their feet. Tom reached into his pocket for the piece of the amulet. Then he took hold of the leather cord around his neck, on which the first piece hung, and fitted the second piece to it. Elenna touched his hand.

"What's that on the surface?" she asked, pointing at the silver disk. There were faint lines scored into the metal. "What do you think they mean?"

Tom shook his head. "I don't know," he said. "This is one mystery that will have to wait. First, we must track down Equinus." He pulled out his compass and checked the secret clock. The hand was now climbing slowly toward the top.

"We're running out of time," he told Elenna gravely. "And that means time is running out for Storm."

"We need to head farther inward," said Elenna, peering through the tightly packed trees.

Tom heard a faint sound from far away. He and Elenna froze in their tracks and listened hard. Something large and powerful was plowing through the branches and creepers of the dense jungle toward them.

"Equinus!" whispered Elenna.

Tom nodded. "He's found us."

With a roar, the huge Ghost Beast burst out from the trees, his black heart thumping in his transparent chest. Tom and Elenna watched with horrified fascination as Equinus switched from his ghostly form to his flesh-and-blood form, before turning back again with a cold shimmer. The Beast whipped his tail viciously and stamped his hooves, churning up the dust all around him. The bones in his skeletal face stood out sharp as knives.

His evil, blazing eyes glared in hatred at Tom, and Equinus charged straight at him.

CHAPTER EIGHT

DOUBLE TROUBLE

Tom had to think quickly. Now that he had found the second piece of the amulet, he knew he must have lost another gift. He just didn't know which.

"Good thing I still have my super-strength," he called quickly to Elenna. "I'm going to need it. Stay here."

Pushing his doubts aside, he scrambled up onto the recently fallen tree trunk. He had an idea, but he needed to get as high as possible if he was to stand any chance against this terrible Beast. He planted his feet as firmly as he could on the trunk, and its branches quivered and sent a shower of gray dust to the ground. With luck, the tree would hold his weight long enough for him to put his bold plan into action.

As the Beast stormed at him, Tom saw Equinus become solid and his black heart disappeared under his ivory skin. It was clear: Equinus didn't want Tom's life force — he wanted to crush him. Tom smiled to himself. This was exactly what he hoped the Beast would do. By becoming solid, Tom knew that he might be able to wrestle the Beast to the ground. And once he'd done that, he would find a way to plunge his sword into the black heart of the Ghost Beast.

Equinus was almost on top of him now, and at the last possible moment, Tom threw out his arms and grasped at the Beast's torso with all his might. A terrible shock of cold stabbed through him as he fell through the Beast and crashed onto the ground. In that instant, Equinus had taken on his ghostly form once more and, as Tom had passed through him, freezing ice had made him shudder. The ice-cold feeling seeped up his arms and threatened to take over his whole body. Tom realized that the Ghost Beast was in fact trying to take away his life force. He summoned up all his strength of heart and climbed to his feet, ignoring the trembling that shook his body as he felt his energies draining away. He saw Equinus begin to turn back into his solid form. This was Tom's chance! He threw himself at the Beast, wrapping his arms around his enemy's body. Equinus gave a scream of anger and pain.

As the Beast writhed, Tom gave a violent twist, using his arms to yank Equinus to one side. The Beast stumbled and fell to the ground, dragging Tom with him.

Tom landed heavily, and lay choking in the dust. His eyes streamed in the gritty air. He spotted the blurry shape of Elenna's hand leaning down toward him. He grasped it gratefully and felt her pulling

him to his feet. But as he wiped his eyes quickly on his sleeve, he heard a sharp, desperate howl and saw Equinus rise up from the dust, hooves flailing.

"Look out, Elenna!" Tom shouted in warning.

Elenna staggered back, but she was looking openmouthed at the Ghost Beast. "He's changing!"

Tom stared in disbelief. Elenna was right. Equinus was transforming, but not to his ghostly form this time. The cold ivory tone of his skin was changing as a faint flesh color spread over his head, neck, and chest. His ashen-gray horse body and legs were becoming a vivid, shining chestnut.

"Tom, by holding on to him, you did something. I don't think he can turn into a ghost anymore!" exclaimed Elenna.

"My strength of heart must have given me the power to stand up to him when he tried to steal my life force," Tom replied. "Thank goodness I didn't lose *that* gift!" *But which gift have I lost?* he thought.

"What do we do next?" Elenna whispered.

"We fight him," Tom replied defiantly, drawing his sword. "It'll be a fairer fight now that he can't change."

A horrible ripping noise filled the air. Before their eyes, Equinus became two separate beings. In a flash, a huge manlike creature, covered in coarse bristles, was standing firm on new human legs. He was dressed in a hemp tunic and leggings, and by his side a giant horse stamped his hooves and tossed his head wildly. The Beast's yellow eyes flashed angrily. He was ready to attack. Now they had two enemies to face — and defeat — if they were to save Storm!

Equinus gave a roar of laughter. It was harsh and sounded like the cracking of rock.

"Death comes in two parts!" he jeered. "Dare you follow?" He turned and disappeared into the jungle. They heard him crashing through the undergrowth.

"You're not getting away that easily!" shouted Elenna. She gave chase. "I'll stop him," she yelled over her shoulder at Tom. "You deal with that horse."

Tom studied the animal. The Beast's eyes were rolling in his head, his breath coming in panicked snorts, and foam spraying from his mouth. Tom leaped onto a nearby rock and vaulted onto the horse's back. He reared and bucked, trying to throw him off, but Tom squeezed his legs around the horse's flanks and held on to the Beast's chestnut mane. If things continued like this, the horse would tire himself out, and that was exactly what Tom wanted.

The horse soon began to pant, and Tom gave a silent cheer of victory. The Beast suddenly paused and then charged at a tree. A low-hanging branch rammed into Tom's midriff, knocking him off the horse. He landed on his feet but was winded. He fumbled for his sword. This needed to end now.

Elenna was all on her own against the other part of the Beast.

The horse charged toward him. Raising the sword high, Tom brought the hilt down against the Beast's sweating temple with all of his magic strength. With a tremendous crash, the horse collapsed into the dust, unconscious.

Now to find Elenna. Tom knew she was strong and brave, but Equinus was a devious Beast. He followed the trail that the Beast had left in the dust on the jungle floor. He sped between the trees, dodging huge, dry leaves and clinging creepers. He didn't want to imagine how little time might be left on the special clock in his compass. All he knew was that he had to destroy Equinus as soon as he could to restore Storm's life force.

Bursting through a clump of ferns, he found Elenna and Equinus. The Beast was pinned to a tree by one of her arrows. The point had gone through the hemp of his tunic and he seemed to be stuck fast. Elenna stood with another arrow ready to fire if Equinus moved. Tom kept his sword in his hand just in case. Elenna didn't take her eyes off the Beast, but she gave Tom a grin of welcome. "I went hunting and look what I found," she said.

"Nice work," Tom said.

The sight of Tom seemed to enrage Equinus and give him new strength. In an instant, he had torn himself free from the tree and grabbed Elenna. He spun her around and snatched away her bow and arrow.

Elenna tried to wrench them back. But with a thrust of his arm, Equinus flung her to the ground. And before Tom could go to her aid, the Beast had pulled back on the bow and was pointing an arrow directly at Tom's heart.

→ CHAPTER NINE →

THE FINAL BATTLE

TOM STARED AT THE DEADLY SHARP POINT OF the arrow. He had never thought he would find himself facing one of his friend's weapons.

Holding the Beast's gaze and keeping his face blank to hide his intent, Tom suddenly hurled his sword through the air. The flat blade flew in an arc and smacked against the Beast's hands, and with a cry of pain Equinus lost his grip on Elenna's bow and arrow. They fell to the ground, along with Tom's sword. Quick as lightning, Elenna snatched them up and threw Tom his sword.

Equinus turned his mighty head this way and that, desperately looking for another weapon. He reached up and ripped a huge branch from the tree above. He swished it menacingly about his head.

Tom weighed his sword in his hand. It felt good. He stepped forward to face Equinus. He would fight until the end. Storm's life depended on him.

With a roar, the Beast swung his makeshift club viciously at Tom's head. Tom ducked the blow nimbly. He made a thrust with his sword, but Equinus parried it with the branch, sending a shuddering force through Tom's arm. This enemy was strong. But as Equinus raised the branch above his head, Tom noticed sweat beads on the Beast's face. He felt hope rise inside him. Equinus was not invincible. He was finding the fight took effort.

Tom leaped aside as the branch came swinging toward him again, and he slashed at Equinus, nicking one of the Beast's bristly arms.

"Go, Tom!" Elenna yelled, but he couldn't see her now. Their fight was raising a tornado of dust around them.

The Beast was moving about clumsily in the thick, choking air. He wasn't used to being on two legs, Tom realized. *He may be stronger than me*, he thought. *But I am more agile*.

Tom darted about the clearing, each time avoiding the swing of the vicious club. The Beast was panting and sweating hard now as they fought. But his strength was not diminishing. He swung his weapon in front of him like a battle-ax. Tom found himself having to jump back again and again. *I can't break through his defenses*, Tom thought with frustration. An evil grin played upon the Beast's face as if he had a secret — as if he was sure he would win the deadly contest.

Stepping back to avoid another ferocious swipe of the club, Tom felt his foot slip. He risked a quick look down and utter horror thrilled through him. He was teetering on the edge of a huge, dark pit with sheer sides. Equinus had been very clever. He was pushing Tom toward the drop.

Tom struggled to keep his balance; the ground was slipping from under his feet. Stones and earth were tumbling into the pit, but he didn't hear them hit anything. The pit was bottomless. Tom knew for certain he had no gifts to protect him from an endless fall.

With a smirk of victory, the Beast lunged at Tom, using his club like a sword. For one terrible moment, Tom could feel that he was toppling backward and slipping over the edge of the pit.

"Not while there's blood in my veins!" he yelled defiantly, and he propelled his body forward and regained his balance. Then he saw his chance. As Equinus lunged at him once more, Tom ducked beneath the club and threw himself as hard as he could at the Beast's legs.

Now Equinus was completely off balance. With a cry that echoed around the jungle, he stumbled over Tom's diving body and toppled headlong into the pit. As he did so, he thrust out a hand to grab Tom's ankle, but Tom rolled out of the way of the grasping fingers.

The Beast gave a cry that became fainter and fainter as he plunged downward. And when the dust from their fight had settled and Tom peered over the edge, he couldn't see anything — only a great, gaping black hole.

Equinus was swallowed up by the darkness. Had Tom defeated the Beast?

CHAPTER TEN

SAVED!

"Tom!" Elenna rushed to his side. "Thank goodness you're all right! I couldn't see you, but I could hear the fight. It sounded so terrible."

"It was," Tom said grimly. "But it's over now. With any luck, Equinus has gone for good." He hoped he was right. Then he felt a great surge of relief as the outline of a tall figure appeared in the air. "Elenna, look!" He pointed over Elenna's shoulder. She turned, and before them stood an image of Taladon. Right away Tom could see that his father looked more solid.

"Well done," Taladon said, and the light around him made Tom feel warm, just as it had done before. "I cannot thank you both enough. As soon as you retrieved the piece of amulet, I felt new strength returning to me."

"Equinus has gone," said Tom. "But what of the horse? I brought him down, but I didn't see what happened to the Beast after that."

"You need not fear," Taladon told him. "The horse turned to dust when you defeated Equinus. You have fulfilled your Quest. Now you must make haste. There is another who wishes to thank you."

"Storm!" Elenna said with a gasp.

Quickly, Tom flicked open his compass to look at the hidden clock. The hand was now moving backward.

"Storm's safe!" Tom cried.

His father smiled. "Not just Storm," he said. "Everyone touched by the evil of Equinus has been returned to their former lives. Thanks to you." Taladon saluted them and his image slowly faded.

Tom felt his heart leap with joy. They had found

the amulet piece and saved his beloved horse. This Quest was over.

"Let's get to Storm!" he yelled, and he began to run through the trees.

"Hold on!" Elenna exclaimed. "We've gone a long way through the jungle and I'm not sure our tracks will be clear enough to follow. Which way do we go?"

Tom held out his hand. "Map," he called. It appeared immediately in the air in front of them. Tom skidded to a halt and looked eagerly at it. A line on the ghostly map's surface materialized and showed them the way out of the jungle.

"And look. Storm's right at the end of our path!" Tom exclaimed. "Come on!"

This time Elenna didn't try to stop him. The two friends didn't stop running until they burst out onto the plain.

"There's the oak tree!" yelled Elenna.

"And there's Storm!" cried Tom happily. "And Silver!"

The two friends sprinted across the dusty earth to meet their faithful animals. Silver yelped in delight, and Tom untied his horse's reins from the tree and flung his arms around Storm's neck before burying his face in his mane. He gazed intently into Storm's brown eyes. They were sparkling and full of life. Tom laughed with relief. Silver ran around them, howling happily.

"Thank you, Silver," said Elenna, crouching down to greet him. "I knew we could trust you to guard Storm."

As if he understood, Silver rubbed his head against Storm's leg, and Storm put his nose down to nuzzle his friend.

Then Tom heard his father's voice in the air. "Are you sure you are ready for your next Quest, my brave warriors?" Taladon said.

"We are," chorused Tom and Elenna eagerly.

"Good," said Taladon's voice, and Tom could hear that his father was pleased. "Then you have to journey to the Dead Peaks. Rashouk is the Beast you must fight there if you are to reclaim the next piece of the amulet. But beware. Rashouk is a troll, and one of Malvel's most terrifying Beasts. He has great cunning. You will need all your skills if you are to succeed. But there is one that I am afraid you have lost — the power granted by the golden gauntlets — your special sword skills."

With that, the voice faded.

Tom stood back from Storm. "A new Beast," he murmured, fingering the pieces of amulet under his shirt. "Will I be able to defeat another of Malvel's creatures without my sword skills?"

"You have many more skills than the magic ones that you've been given," Elenna told him. "I know you can do anything you put your mind to."

Tom gave Storm a loving pat on the neck and turned to Elenna.

"There's only one way to find out," he declared. "On with the Quest!"

TOM'S QUEST CONTINUES WITH . . .

BEASTQUEST

AMULET OF AVANTIA

→ BOOK TWENTY-ONE ←

RASHOUK
THE CAVE TROLL

READ A SNEAK PEEK HERE!

ESCAPING THE DEAD JUNGLE

"ALMOST THERE!" SAID TOM, AS HE SWUNG his sword at the last section of wild overgrowth blocking their path out of the Forbidden Land's Dead Jungle.

"Great," said Elenna, as she led Tom's stallion, Storm, out onto the flat grassland. "I thought we'd never get out."

Storm whinnied in delight. Close behind, Elenna's pet wolf, Silver, yelped and ran around in wide circles.

Tom laughed and sheathed his sword. "I think they're happy they can stretch their legs again!"

"Although, to be fair, this place isn't exactly cheery," said Elenna, looking around at the dead grassland that stretched as far as the eye could see. "I never knew that anywhere in Avantia could look so dead and depressing."

"Me, neither," said Tom, thinking of the beauty of the rest of the kingdom and how the Dark Wizard, Malvel, had tried more than once to destroy it. It was because of Malvel that Tom was on his current Quest. The Dark Wizard had turned Tom's father, Taladon, into a ghost, and Tom had to find the six pieces of the Amulet of Avantia to make his father flesh and blood again. Malvel had scattered the broken pieces of the amulet around the kingdom's Forbidden Land, where they were guarded by six Ghost Beasts — evil creatures who could switch from real to ghostly form in an instant.

Tom had already defeated two of them and retrieved two pieces of the amulet. He vowed to overcome the next four Beasts as well — though he would have to do so without some of the magical powers he possessed.

On his previous Quests, he had retrieved all six pieces of Avantia's golden armor. Each piece had given him a different power, although Tom didn't need to be wearing the armor to use them.

But the armor did not belong to him. It belonged to his father. And now, every time Tom recovered a piece of the amulet, one of the armor's magical powers returned to Taladon.

Tom frowned as a feeling of disquiet spread through him. He had already lost the powers granted him by the golden boots and the golden gauntlets. It appeared that he was losing his powers in the reverse order to which he had gained them. Therefore, if he succeeded in defeating the next Ghost Beast, Rashouk the Cave Troll, he would probably lose the power of the leg armor and would no longer have his increased speed.

"Which way shall we ride?" asked Elenna, snapping Tom out of his thoughts.

"Map!" he commanded, stretching out a hand.

The air shimmered as a ghostly map appeared before his eyes. It was a gift from Aduro, the good wizard, to help them navigate the Forbidden Land.

Elenna joined him to study the map. "Look," she said, pointing at some mountains in the east called the Dead Peaks. "Didn't your father say we'd find Rashouk there?"

Tom nodded. He wondered how it would be to do battle with Rashouk now that he'd lost two of his powers.

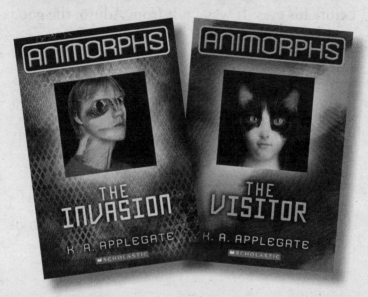